Contents

characters created by lauren child

MY extremely GOOD story collection

PUFFIN

PUFFIN BOOKS
Published by the Penguin Group: London, New York, Australia,
Canada, India, Ireland, New Zealand and South Africa
Penguin Books Ltd, Registered Offices: 80 Strand, London WC2R 0RL, England

puffinbooks.com

But I Am An Alligator, I Want To Be Much More Bigger Like You, I Can't Stop Hiccuping
and *Help! I Really Mean It!* first published in Great Britain in Puffin Books 2010
I Can Do Anything That's Everything All On My Own and *You Can Be My Friend*
first published in Great Britain in Puffin Books 2008
This collection published in Puffin Books 2012
001 – 10 9 8 7 6 5 4 3 2 1

Made and printed in China

ISBN: 978-0-718-19896-1

But I AM an alligator

Text based on the script written by Bridget Hurst

Illustrations from the TV animation produced by Tiger Aspect

I have this little sister Lola.

She is small and very funny.

One thing Lola loves is dressing up.

"This is my favourite fancy dress costume and I'm not ever NEVER taking it off," says Lola.

Then Lola says,
"Did you know
all-i-gators live in
swamps and rivers
where they are very
difficult to see?

That's because they are
ca-moo-flarged.

And, you know,
alligators lay eggs,
not babies.

"And sometimes they grow
BIGGER
than even our table!"
says Lola.

"So you see, Charlie,
alligators are really
very interesting.
That's why I am
going to wear my
alligator costume
ALL the time."

So I say,
"ALL the time, Lola?"

And she says,
"Yes, Charlie.
I'm not taking it off ever!
NEVER!"

When Mum takes us
shopping, Lola says,
"I want to eat what
all-i-gators eat."

I say,
"I don't think they eat
frozen prawns, Lola."

But Lola shouts,
"Oh, they absolutely
do, Charlie!
Alligators LOVE
frozen prawns!"

And I say,
"Shhh, Lola. Everyone's looking at us."

At the park,
Lola is STILL wearing her
alligator costume.

Marv says,
"Have you asked her
to take it off?"

So I say,
"A gazillion, million times,
but she says
she is going to
wear it FOREVER!"

And Marv says,
"Well, she can't
wear it to school, can she?"

And I say, "NO! She
can't wear it to school!"

"Of course
I am going to wear it
to **school**," says Lola.

And I say,
"I really don't think
it's such a good idea.
Won't your friends
think wearing
an **alligator costume**
is a bit **strange**?"

Lola says,
"No, Charlie.
I think they will all want
alligator costumes,
too. Especially when
I do my **talk**."

So I say,
"YOUR TALK?"

And Lola says,
"Yes, Charlie!
We have to do a talk in
assembly tomorrow.
It's called
'All About Me'."

Then I say,
"But you are
NOT an alligator, Lola.
Don't you think it
would be better
if you tell the whole
school about YOU,
dressed as YOU?
You could tell
them about...

how you like
drawing...
... and how you
always hop into bed...

... and how
pink milk
is your
favourite and
your best."

Lola says,
"That would not
be very interesting.
Everybody
already knows I like
pink milk!"

And so I say,
"I could help you
with your talk,
if you like."

But Lola says,
"I do not need any help."

At assembly the next day,
Lola says,
"My name is Lola,
and I like dressing up.

At the moment,
I like dressing up as
an all-i-gator
because it is my most
favourite costume
and it is my best.

"I used to like **dressing** up as a Spanish lady.

Or sometimes as a circus person.

But I could also **dress** up as...

"... a doctor!

Or a caterpillar...

... who turns into
a butterfly."

And the whole school says,
"Wow!"

Lola says,
"I love dressing up,
because I can be whatever
I want to be...
and that is my best."

Everyone cheers.

And I say,
"Well done, Lola!"

The next day,
Lola is not an alligator.
She has whiskers, pointy ears and a tail.
Lola says, "Meow!"
And I say, "Oh no."

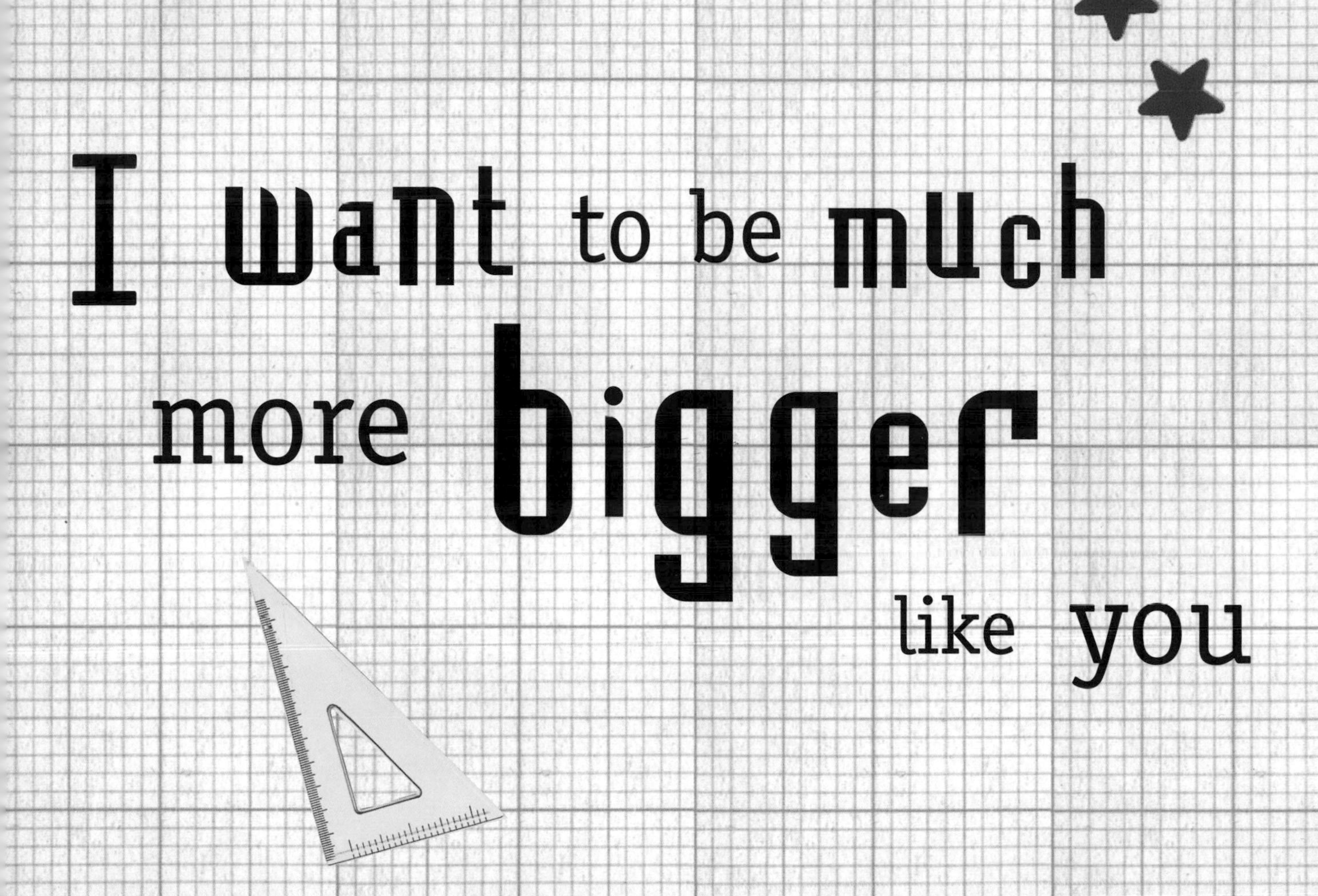
I want to be much
more bigger
like you

Text based on the script written by Carol Noble

Illustrations from the TV animation produced by Tiger Aspect

I have this little sister Lola.
She is small and very funny.
Lola says, "I'm not small, Charlie.
I am getting more **bigger**
and grown-up all of the time."

"And now that I am
much more bigger,
I can go on the
Super-Duper
Loopy Loopy ride."

So I say,
"The Super-Duper
Loop the Looper is
very, very SCARY.
Are you sure?"

"I am very sure, Charlie,"
says Lola.

“Aaaagghh!”

So I measure Lola
to see if she really is
bigger.

"Charlie, I must be
more taller than that!
Are you tricking me?"

"No, Lola. That's exactly
how big you are."

Then Lola says,
"But, I absolutely MUST
be big enough to
go on the Super-Duper
Loopy Loopy ride."

I say, "There are still loads of **fun rides** at the fair for smaller people. The **Chug-a-Bugs** ride is really exciting."

And Lola says, "I don't think so, Charlie."

Then Lola says,
"I have a GOOD plan.
I am going to
think myself bigger.

Now I am thinking
I am nearly as
big as a sunflower
touching the sun...

"And now I am thinking I am as **big** as one of those extremely

T A L L E S T

buildings."

I say,
"You can't MAKE yourself
bigger, Lola.
It just happens."

Lola says,
"It's not fair.
Why am I always, always
the small one?"

So I say,
"There are great
things about
being small. Like...

"... you get **stories**
read to you
every night...

and you get loads of
piggybacks."

But Lola says,
"I still really, **really**
would like being
the **biggest.**"

When Marv comes over,
he says,
"Are you ready for
the Super-Duper
Loop the Looper?"

And Lola shouts,
"I am! I am! I am!"

Then Marv whispers,
"She's quite small for the ride,
isn't she, Charlie?"

And I say,
"Yup."

Charlie

At the fair,
Marv says,
"The **Super-Duper Loop the Looper** is going to be the best ride!"

"Yes. It will make our hair stand on end," I say.

"And our tummies go all **funny**," says Marv. "I can't wait! How about you, Lola?"

"Err… I can't wait either…"

"Aaagghh!"
"Ooohh!"

Charlie

When we get
to the front of the line
Marv says,
"**Hold on** to your
tummy, Lola!"

But Lola says,
"Err... I think
I might be slightly
too small still.

Perhaps it would be
a little more **fun**
if I went on something
for more slightly
smaller people –
like the
Chug-a-Bugs!"

So we all go on the **Chug-a-Bugs**
and Lola **laughs** and **laughs**.
She says, "You were right, Charlie!
The **Chug-a-Bugs** IS the very best ride
in the whole world and the universe."

I can't STOP hiccuping!

Text based on
the script written by
David Ingham
Illustrations from
the TV animation
produced by
Tiger Aspect

I have this little sister Lola.
She is small and very funny.
Lola is practising the words to her song.
She is **singing** it with Lotta tonight
at the school **concert**.

Lola and Lotta **sing**,

"The spring is here,
the cold has fled.
The flowers bloom
and raise their heads.

Spring is here!
Spring is here!
Spring is here at last!"

Then Lola and Lotta
giggle...
and giggle...
until – *HIC!* –
Lola **hiccups**!

In art class,
Lola paints a bird
with a big tail
and a teeny, tiny beak.

HIC!

When Lola **hiccups**,
her brush flies
across the painting.

Arnold says,
"Now it looks like
an aeroplane."

Lola says,
"But I didn't want to –
HIC! – paint an aeroplane."

At breaktime, Lola says,
"My hiccups won't – *HIC!* –
go away!"

So I say, "I have an idea.
Look at my finger
very, very closely."

Then Marv jumps
out of nowhere.
"BOO!"

Lola screams.
"Why did you do that?"

Marv says,
"To scare away your hiccups."

And Lola says,
"They're completely gone!"

In class, Lola says,
"The concert's going to be
all right now that
my hiccups have
gone away."

Lotta says, "Oh yes.
Do you like my tower?"

Lola leans in
for a closer look.
HIC!

Lola knocks
Lotta's tower over.

Lola says,
"Sorry – *HIC!* – Lotta!"

At lunch, everyone tells Lola different ways to get rid of her **hiccups**.

She **pats** her head and **rubs** her tummy.

She drinks from the **wrong** side of her cup.

She says, "AAHHH!"
for as long as she can.

Then Lola tries lying
on her back and wiggling
her legs in the air.

Lotta asks,
"Is it working?"

And Lola says,
"Yes! They're gone!"

But later,
during our snack...
HIC!
Lola's **hiccups** come back.

"Ohhh..."
Lola says.
"At first, they were funny.
But I don't want
to have them
ANY MORE."

I say,
"Sometimes things
can be fun at first,
but then you can get
a bit fed up.
Like strawberries.
The first one's always
super delicious."

And Lola says,
"But if you
eat too many of them,
they are not fun.
Just like my hiccups."

So I say,
"What hiccups?"

And Lola says,
"They're gone again!"

Lola and Lotta
are backstage
before the school **concert**.

Lola says,
"I haven't **hiccuped**
for nearly
one whole hour."

Lotta says,
"Should we have
one last little practice?"

Lola and Lotta **sing**
their song, and they
giggle and giggle.
Then, *HIC!*

Lola says,
"Oh no! *HIC!*
We'd better get Charlie."

Lola says,
"Lotta made me – *HIC!* –
laugh, and I got
the hiccups again.
How can I – *HIC!* – sing
with the hiccups?"

So I say,
"Try making ME laugh
so I can catch your hiccups.
Then you won't
have them!"

Lola wiggles and
makes silly faces.
Lotta blows a raspberry.

I say,
"Hee hee hee... *HIC!*"

Onstage, Lotta and Lola
sing their song.

"The spring is here,
the cold has fled.
The flowers bloom
and raise their heads.

Spring is here!
Spring is here!
Spring is here at last!"

Lola sings the song
without even
one little hiccup!
Everyone claps,
especially me and Marv.

Marv asks, "How did you do it?"
I say, "I pretended Lola had given her **hiccups** to me."
We laugh, and all of a sudden I... *HIC!*
Marv says, "Very funny, Charlie."
I say, "*HIC!* Now I really have the **hiccups**!"

HELP!

I really mean it!

Text based on the script written by Anna Starkey

Illustrations from the TV animation produced by Tiger Aspect

I have this little sister Lola.

She is small and very funny.

Today we are looking after Caspar,

Granny and Grandpa's cat.

Lola REALLY loves Caspar.

Charlie

Lola says,

"Look, Charlie!

Caspar is playing

a game with us."

So I say,

"Caspar is a cat.

He might not like

all of your games."

"Hc dcfinitely

likes this one," says Lola.

Then Lola says,

"Lotta, did you know

that Caspar is an

actual tiger..."

"Oooh! Lola,
what are those noises?"
asks Lotta.

Lola says,
"I don't know.
But it's all right because
we are with Caspar.

Oh...
where's Caspar gone?"

And Lotta says, "Oh! Yes!
Where's Caspar gone?"

Then Lola and Lotta shout,
"HEEEELLLLPPPPP!"

Me and Marv run in
and ask,
"Are you all right?!"

And Lola says,
"Yes, Charlie!
Caspar was just going to
rescue me and Lotta
from some tigers."

So I say,
"Lola, you must ONLY
call for help
if you REALLY mean it."

And Lola says,
"Sorry, Charlie.
We only said HELP
by accident."

Lotta says,
"It was very funny
when we said HELP
and Charlie and Marv
came running in."

And Lola asks,
"Do you think
if we say help now,
they will come in
again?"

"HELP! HELP!
HELP! HELP!"

"What's the matter?!"
me and Marv ask.

And Lola says,
"Nothing, Charlie..."

So I say,
"Oh. I get it.
Very funny."

"We won't do it again,"
says Lola.

So I ask,
"Do you promise?"

And Lola says,
"We absolutely
do promise."

Later, Lotta says,
"Look! Caspar
likes dressing up.

Do you think cats
like wearing hats?"

"Oh! I know they do,"
says Lola.
"And they like going
for carriage rides, too.

Come on, Caspar.
It's time for a ride."

"Caspar, where are you?"

"Are you here, Caspar?"

"Caspar! Where are you?"

"Caspar!

CASPAR!"

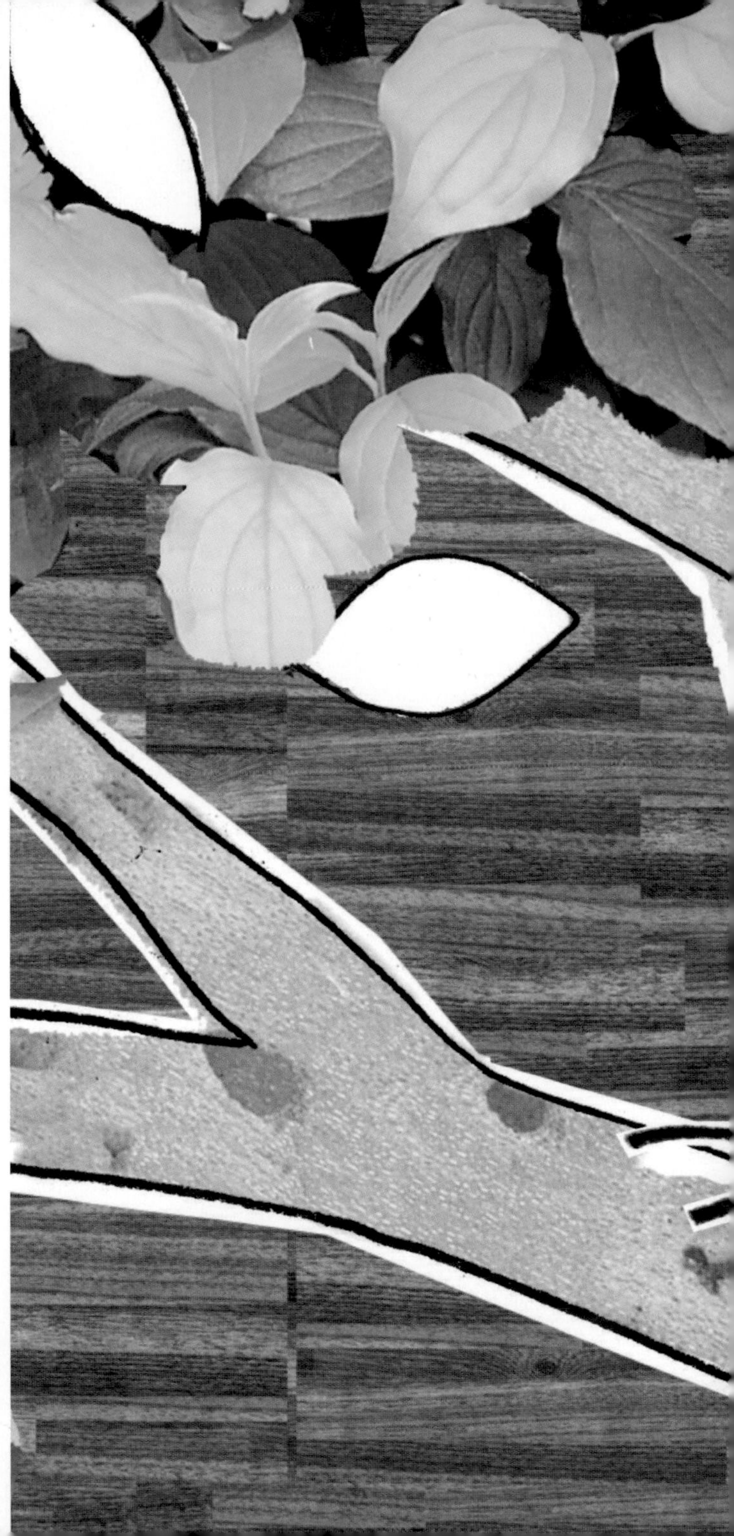

"Oh no!
HELP, Charlie! HELP!"

And I ask, "What is it
this time, Lola?"

Lola says,
"Caspar's stuck
right up in the sky,
and he's crying and his
hat's gone all wonky!"

So I say,
"Sorry, Lola.
It's not going to
work this time."

And Lola says,
"But Charlie,
we really, REALLY
need you to help..."

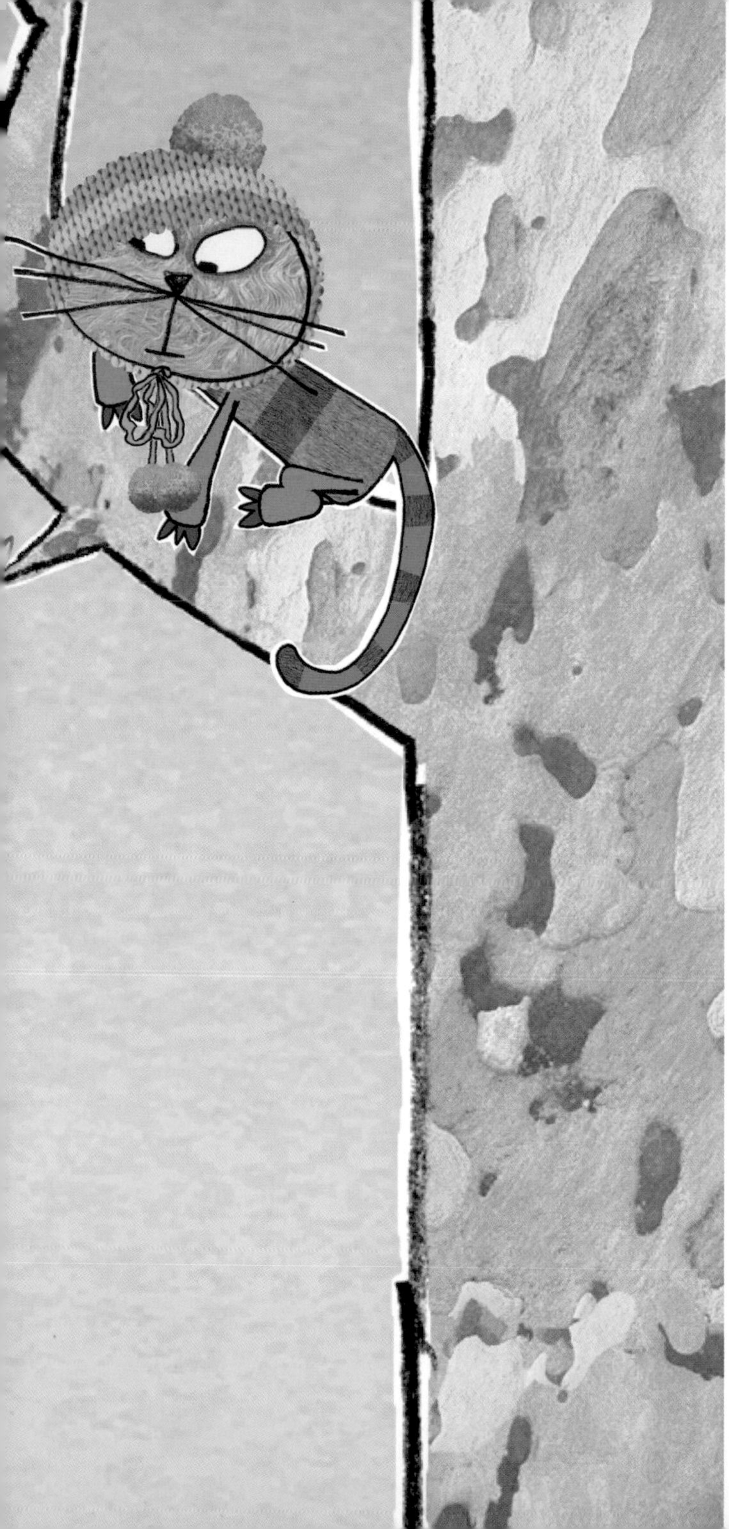

"Charlie and Marv
don't believe me
so we've got to get Caspar
down by ourselves.
Please come down, Caspar!"

And Lotta says, "PLEASE!"

Then Caspar climbs
higher up the tree.

And Lola shouts,
"Noooooo!
Charlie! HELP!"

Me and Marv run over
and Lola says,
"See? I did **really** need you."

And I say, "But I didn't
believe you because
you kept **shouting** HELP
when you didn't mean it."

Lola and Lotta say,
"Sorry, Charlie.
Sorry, Marv."

And I say,
"Look! Caspar has **jumped**
on to Marv's balcony!"

charlie

Then Marv says, "Err... Charlie,
why is that **cat** wearing a **hat**?"
So I say, "**Cats** don't like **hats**, Lola."
And Marv says,
"I would run away, too, if I had to wear a **hat** like that!"

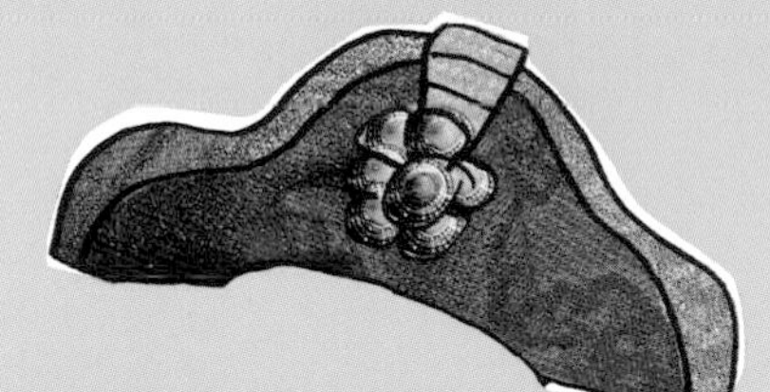

I CAN do anything

that's everything

ALL on my own

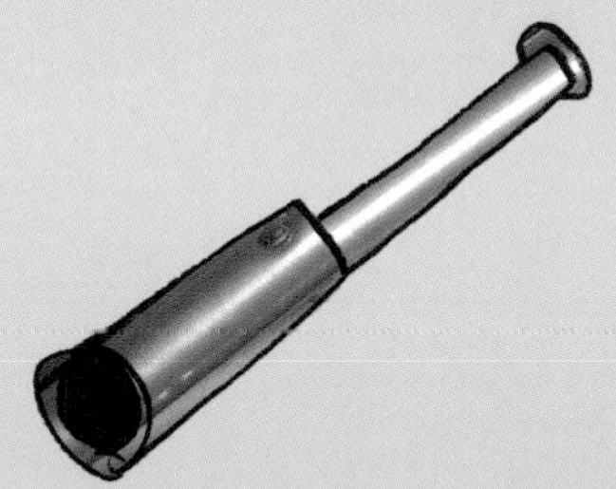

Text based on the script written by
Carol Noble & Bridget Hurst

Illustrations from the TV animation
produced by Tiger Aspect

I have this little sister Lola.
She is small and very funny.
At the moment, Lola likes to say,
"I can do anything that's everything
ALL on my own."

"whOooops"

Lola says,
"I can button up my coat
ALL on my own.

I can use the computer
ALL on my own.

And I can DEFINITELY
pour pink milk
ALL on my own."

I say, "Let me **help**, Lola."

But she says, "NO.
I can do **anything**
that's **everything**
ALL on my **own**."

So then I say,
"Lola, **helping** is
VERY important.

What about the
milk monkeys
in the jungle?

How do you think
they get their
pink milk?

"They HELP each other!

If the monkeys
tried to do this
ALL on their own,
they would
NEVER get their
pink milk."

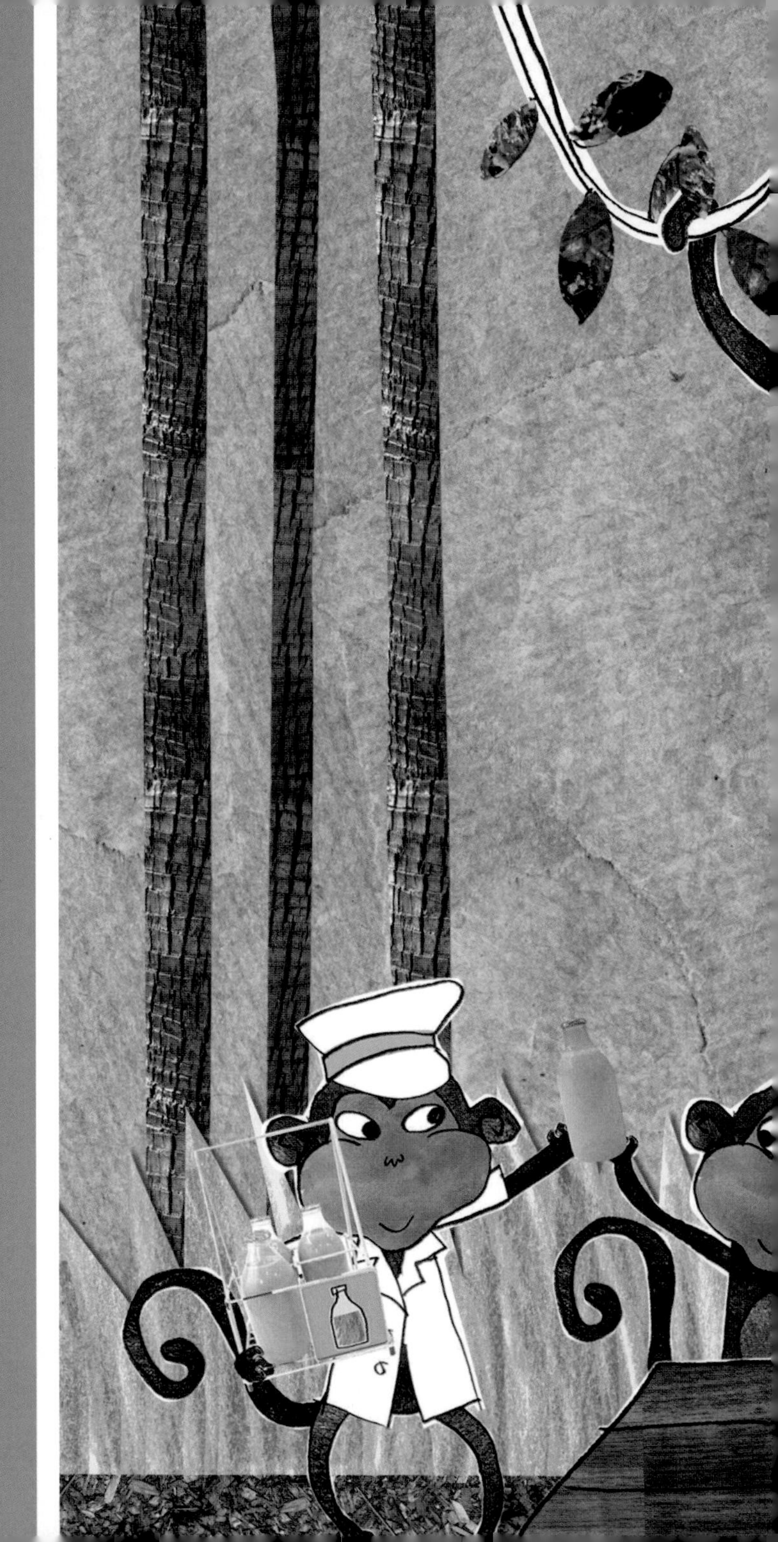

"But I am NOT
a monkey
so I do not need
any help,"
says Lola.

"I can do anything
that's everything
ALL on my own."

charlie

Char

Later,
Marv and Lola and me
go to the park.

Marv says,
"Lola, do you want
to play piggy
in the middle?"

And Lola says,
"NO thank you.

I am going to
the playground to swing
ALL on my own."

Charlie

Then I say,
"Hey, Lola. Do you want
to play with us?"

She says,
"NO thank you, Charlie.

Next I will be playing
on the see-saw
ALL on my own."

Then Marv says,
"But the see-saw
will not SEE or SAW
with only one person."

And I say, "Yes.
You need two people
to go up in the air."

But Lola says,
"Why would I want
to go high up
when I can see
LOTS of interesting things
very close and near
to the ground?"

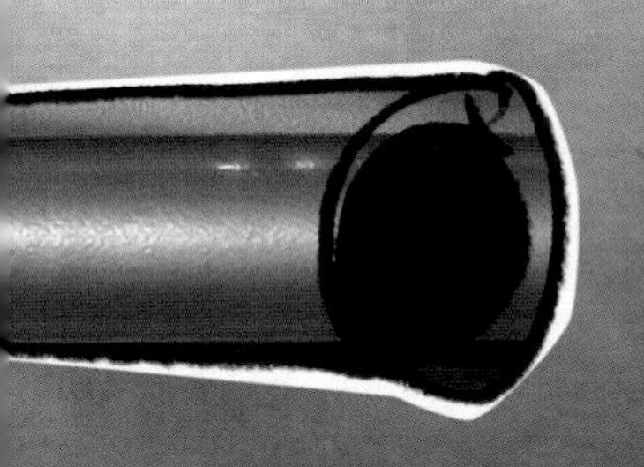

So I say, "But Lola,
being high up
can be REALLY fantastic."

Then Marv and me
get on the see-saw
and Lola goes high up
in the air.

I say, "What can you see,
Captain Lola?"

"I can see a
GIANT octopus," says Lola,
"And I can see...

"... PIRATES!
And they are coming
to get us!"

We shout, "HELP!
Captain Lola! HELP!"

"Don't worry, Charlie!
Don't worry, Marv!
I will rescue you."

Then Lola says,
"See, Charlie?
I saved you
AND Marv from the
EVER-so-mean pirates.

You couldn't
untie yourselves
on your own,
could you?

I can do anything
that's everything
ALL on my own!"

arlie

And I say, "Yes, Lola. You CAN do everything all on your own... except WALK home."

And do you know what Lola says then?

"Oh, Charlie, walking home isn't any fun

ALL on my own."

YOU

can be my

friend

Text based on the script written by Carol Noble
Illustrations from the TV animation
produced by Tiger Aspect

I have this little sister Lola.
She is small and very funny.
Today Lola is excited because
Marv is coming over and he is
bringing his little brother Morten.

Lola says,
"Me and Morten
are going to do
LOTS of things together,
like have a tea party!

I LOVE having tea parties.
And dressing up!
Everyone LOVES
dressing up."

Then I say,
"If you run out
of things to do,
Morten really likes playing
Round-and-Round."

But Lola says,
"Oh no!
I really do not like
Round-and-Round.

All you do is
go round
and round...
and round.
Nothing happens, Charlie."

Then the doorbell rings
and Lola shouts,
"MORTEN'S HERE!"

Lola says,
"Hello, Morten."

Morten doesn't
say **anything**.

So Marv says,
"Morten's not really
a big talker."

And Lola says,
"Morten, do you
want to see my room?"

But Morten still
doesn't say **anything**.

Lola says,
"Would you like
a cup of tea, Morten?"

Morten just stares.

So then she asks,
"Would you like a biscuit?"

Not a peep from Morten.

"Oh," says Lola.
"Well, what we'll
do now is...

"... dressing up!
Look at me, Morten.
I'm a mermaid.

Morten, you can be
a pirate."

But Morten
just stands there.

So Lola says,
"I know!
Let's pretend we live
in Upside Down."

Lola says,
"In Upside Down,
absolutely everything
is completely
¡umop apısdn

Would you like
a tea of cup, Morten?
That's Upside Down
for 'cup of tea'!"

Morten doesn't even move.

So Lola shouts,
"Morten! Don't you
want to play?"

Morten just shakes his head.

Later, Lola whispers,
"Morten didn't like any of my games, Charlie. He didn't even talk to me."

So I say,
"Marv told you, Morten isn't really a big talker."

Then Lola says,
"But he didn't even say one SINGLE word. He doesn't like me."

Then Lola sighs and blows some bubbles in her pink milk.

And do you know what?
Morten starts giggling.

"Hee hee hee hee hee hee."

Then Morten tries blowing
pink milk bubbles.

Lola and Morten
giggle some more.

Then Lola says,
"I know! I know!
Next let's play
bubbles outside.

Morten, what do you
think it would be like
to be inside a bubble?"

"Bubbly," says Morten.

"I looooove
being in a bubble,"
says Lola.

And Morten says,
"I love being
in a bubble, too."

arlie

Later, we all have
tea at Marv and
Morten's flat.
Lola and Morten
can't stop **giggling** and
whispering together.

Morten asks,
"Would you like to
play a game, Lola?
It's called
Round-and-Round!"

Lola looks unsure
so I say, "Go on, Lola."

And Lola says,
"OK, Charlie. But only
because Morten is my
new special **friend**."

Morten says,
"Your turn, Lola! What you do is…"
"I know," says Lola. "You go round
and round and round…
and round."